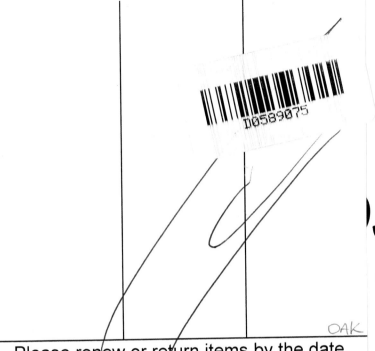

Please renew or return items by the date shown on your receipt

www.hertsdirect.org/libraries

Renewals and enquiries: 0300 123 4049

Textphone for hearing or speech impaired 0300 123 4041

'**Preposterous Rhinoceros'**
An original concept by Tracy Gunaratnam
© Tracy Gunaratnam

Illustrated by Marta Costa

Published by MAVERICK ARTS PUBLISHING LTD

Studio 3A, City Business Centre, 6 Brighton Road,

Horsham, West Sussex, RH13 5BB

© Maverick Arts Publishing Limited August 2015

+44 (0)1403 256941

A CIP catalogue record for this book is available at the British Library.

ISBN 978-1-84886-180-0

www.maverickbooks.co.uk

This book is rated as: Turquoise Band
The original picture book text for this story has been modified
by the author to be an early reader.

PREPOSTEROUS
RHINOCEROS

by Tracy Gunaratnam
illustrated by Marta Costa

The animals were getting ready for a bedtime story when...

"Disaster!" yelled Drama Llama.

"King Lion has lost his voice! Who
will read us a story?"

"Shy Salamander can read,"

snapped Cranky Crocodile.

"She's too shy," said Rhinoceros.

"But I'll read to you!"

"That's preposterous, Rhinoceros!" said everyone.

"You don't know anything about books."

"I know that when the king opens a book, he can tell a story," said Rhinoceros.

The animals were too tired to argue.

Rhinoceros turned to the first page and waited.

He waited and waited and waited.

Nothing happened.

Then he took a key from his pocket.

Perhaps I can wind the book up, he

thought, but that didn't help!

So he shook it and shook it until

the pages fell out!

The animals groaned. There would

be no bedtime story tonight.

The next morning Rhinoceros said, "I need some storytelling advice!"

And he charged off, deep into the jungle.

"Hello, Drama Llama," said Rhinoceros.

"Do you know how to use a book?"

"Just open it and dive straight in,"

Drama Llama replied.

Rhinoceros put the book at the base of

a tall rock, and he climbed up, up, up,

all the way to the very top.

Then he dived head first into the book. Smash!

"That's preposterous, Rhinoceros!"

said Shy Salamander.

"I need some proper advice!" said Rhinoceros, and he charged deeper into the jungle.

"Excuse me, Tiny Toucan," said Rhinoceros,

"Do you know how to use a book?"

"Just open it and get stuck in,"

Tiny Toucan replied.

So Rhinoceros covered himself in sticky honey, and got stuck in.

"That's preposterous, Rhinoceros!" sighed Shy Salamander.

The jungle animals laughed their socks off.

"It's not funny!" said Rhinoceros.

Shy Salamander made the

loudest noise she could.

"RHINOCEROS!!!"

"Books don't need keys, tall rocks or

sticky honey! They just need to be READ!"

"RED!" said Rhinoceros.

"Why didn't you say so?"

"Not that sort of red," said Shy Salamander.

"Come on, I'll show you."

Learning to read was tricky,

but it was fun. Eventually...

wrosd
aer
amgi

words
are
magic

Rhinoceros was ready to read the bedtime story. He opened the book and...

RRROOOAAARRR!

King Lion had found his voice. "Hooray!"

cheered the animals.

"You'll need this," Rhinoceros sighed, giving King Lion the book.

"Wait!" said King Lion. "It's time someone read ME a bedtime story!"

Rhinoceros grinned happily as he read

his favourite story right to the end.

Quiz

1. What does Rhino use to make him 'sticky'?
a) Treacle
b) Honey
c) Jam

2. Why can't Lion read the bedtime story?
a) He has lost his voice
b) He has gone on holiday
c) He is busy

3. Why does salamander not read the story?
a) She's shy
b) She can't read
c) She doesn't like reading

4. Words are _____

a) Difficult

b) Awesome

c) Magic

5. What colour does Rhino try to paint the book?

a) Red

b) Black

c) Blue

Turn over for answers

Maverick Early Readers

Our early readers have been adapted from the original picture books so that children can make the essential transition from listener to reader.

All of these books have been book banded to the industry standard and edited by a leading educational consultant.

Quiz Answers:

1b, 2a, 3a, 4c, 5.